The Magic Sandcastle

SANDCASTLE COMPETITION

Only items found on the beach to be used.
No grown ups allowed to help.
Prizes for best castles.

Serenity Press Pty Ltd
Waikiki, WA 6169

First published by Serenity Press (Serenity Press Kids) in 2021
www.serenitypress.org

National Library of Australia
Cataloguing-in-Publication entry

Clare Milford Haven, The Magic Sandcastle

ISBN: 978-0-6452183-2-9 (hc)
ISBN: 978-0-6452183-4-3 (sc)
ISBN: 978-0-6452183-3-6 (e)

I dedicate this book to my wonderful children who are the main characters in The Magic Sandcastle.

Also to my darling Mother, Granny Annie, without whom we would never have gone to Nantucket. She introduced us to this magical island and brought all the family together there every year, giving us so many happy memories to treasure, including my wedding on the beach in 1997.

Every summer Mr & Mrs Fairchild take
their five children to the seaside.

Their favourite place in the world is
Nantucket, a small island famous for
its whaling history and wide, sandy
beaches, where Granny Fairchild has a
summer house.

Granny Fairchild's house sits at the top of a very steep hill overlooking the harbour.

Every morning, the children look through a pair of their Grandpa's huge old wartime binoculars to see what new boats have come into the harbour.

There are so many different types of boats: boats for fishing, sailing, and some huge ones just for doing nothing!

On hot, sunny days, Granny drives
the children to their favourite
beach called Ladies Beach.

One day, they see a notice about a sandcastle competition to be judged the following day.

"ONLY ITEMS FOUND ON THE BEACH CAN BE USED, AND NO GROWN-UPS ARE ALLOWED TO HELP."

How exciting! The children quickly get to work.

SANDCASTLE COMPETITION

Only items found on the beach to be used.
No grown ups allowed to help.
Prizes for best castles.

James is the oldest so he is "Chief Engineer" and gives each of the others a special task.

Louisa fetches buckets of water from the sea.

Harry looks for bits of old fishing net and twigs.

Tatiana is chief shell scourer, and Wenty is the architect.

Little by little, the sandcastle takes the shape of a medieval fort with turrets, drawbridge, and moat. The drawbridge is made up from some driftwood and string from an old fishing net.

Finally, the finishing touches are put in place – soldiers made out of "mermaid's purses" washed up on the shore, with mussel shells as shields. The children place the soldiers along the battlements and line up "the enemy" outside the moat.

"We're sure to win," announces James as the sun begins to set and everyone packs up to return home.

That night after a supper of fresh corn and swordfish, the children finally go to sleep.

Harry dreams about their fort.

A battle takes place, the fort is ruined, and many of the soldiers are killed.

He wakes with a start, but drifts quickly back to sleep.

It was only a dream.

The following morning is as bright and sunny
as the day before.

At breakfast where they all tuck into warm
blueberry muffins and pancakes with maple
syrup, Harry tells everyone about his dream.

What if it is true and their fort is destroyed?

Their mother knows how important the
competition is so they all rush to get ready
and pile into the car.

The poor old Jeep rattles along as fast as it can down the dirt roads, and the children run up the little path to the place where they made their sandcastle.

"OH NO!" exclaims James, "Harry was right.
There really has been a terrible battle."

Their fort has been devastated.

"We can't win the competition, now," says
James.

"We have to try," says Tatiana. "Let's start
rebuilding it and do the best we can."

There is no time to waste.

They rush about rebuilding the fort and all breathe big sighs of relief as Louisa places the final bucket of water in the moat two minutes before judging is due to start.

"This is very original," booms the judge when she comes to the Fairchild children's entry.

"What is the name of your sandcastle?"

"The Magic Sandcastle," they reply.

"And why is it magic?" she asks.

The children look at each other.

Should they tell her about Harry's dream and what they discovered when they arrived at the beach that morning?

No. She wouldn't believe them.

"It's magic because we believe it is an enchanted fort," says James.

The judge smiles. "How absolutely charming."

She gathers everyone round and announces, "And the winning sandcastle is ... The Magic Sandcastle!"

The children go up to collect their prize – a huge cup filled with vanilla fudge – and grin at each other. If only she knew the fort was truly enchanted!

As they run into the waves, they wonder what might happen to their sandcastle that night, and what other excitements might be in store for the rest of the holidays.

Clare Milford Haven

About the Author

Clare Milford Haven has been writing for the past 30 years, with regular articles published in The Times, Evening Standard, Homes & Gardens and GQ as well as an eight-year stint on Tatler's editorial staff as their Social Editor.

Since the death of her eldest son James in 2006, Clare has devoted her time to the charity she set up in his memory, James' Place. The first James' Place, in Liverpool, was opened by HRH The Duke of Cambridge in June 2018. For further details, please visit the website: www.jamesplace.org.uk

Clare wrote The Magic Sandcastle some years ago, but filed it away, and only dug it out during lockdown in 2020. Clare's mother, 'Granny Annie', was American and bought a house on Nantucket Island in the '60s. The extended family traditionally spend every summer there.

Nantucket has only the happiest of memories for Clare and her family and she wanted to record those memories in the form of a children's book. She also married her husband George Milford Haven on a beach there in August 1997, so it is a place that is very dear to her heart.

The five main characters in the book are Clare's children James, Wenty and Louisa and her stepchildren Tatiana and Harry. When they were small, they spent most of their days on the beach in Nantucket, riding the waves and building sandcastles, so there was unlimited inspiration for the content of the book.

Clare lives in the UK on a farm in Hampshire with her husband George and their four children.